The
STARLIGHT
CLOAK

retold by

Jenny Nimmo
pictures by Justin Todd

Dial Books for Young Readers

New ⚜ York

First published in the United States 1993
by Dial Books for Young Readers
A Division of Penguin Books USA Inc.
375 Hudson Street
New York, New York 10014

Published in Great Britain by
HarperCollins Publishers Ltd
Text copyright © 1993 by Jenny Nimmo
Pictures copyright © 1993 by Justin Todd
All rights reserved
Printed in Great Britain
First Edition
1 3 5 7 9 10 8 6 4 2

Library of Congress Cataloging in Publication Data
Nimmo, Jenny.
The starlight cloak / retold by Jenny Nimmo
pictures by Justin Todd.—1st ed.
p. cm.
Summary: A princess in Ireland leads a life of misery
until her foster mother reveals magical powers
that change her life forever.
ISBN 0-8037-1508-0
[1. Fairy tales. 2. Ireland—Fiction.]
I. Todd, Justin, ill. II. Title.
PZ8.N573St 1993 [E]—dc20 92-26186 CIP AC

In Ireland, long ago, there lived a fair princess. Her name was Oona, and she was the youngest daughter of King Curucha. When Oona was just a baby, her mother the queen died and so her father sent her away to be cared for by a foster mother.

Oona's childhood was very happy, however, for her foster mother was as kind and loving as any true mother. Oona called her Mother Brigid and would have been content to stay with her forever. But when Oona was fourteen, her father decided she must return to take her place at court.

At that time the countries of Europe were at war with one another. Curucha was a great soldier as well as a king; he had to lead his troops in battle and was often absent from his kingdom. He relied on his elder daughters, Sorcha and Deirdra, to care for Oona and to make her life as comfortable as a royal princess's should be. How mistaken he was.

Sorcha and Deirdra were vain, spiteful girls; they were jealous of their little sister's beauty and had no intention of being kind to her. As soon as the king left the castle, the cruel sisters decided to make Oona their servant. The young girl's life became a misery of sweeping and scrubbing. She was forbidden to leave the castle to walk in the sun, given ragged clothes to wear, and a cold attic room where she would lie awake, sobbing for her dear Mother Brigid who seemed as distant as the stars.

On one of his brief visits home the king came upon Oona trudging along a shadowy corridor.

"You look pale, my child. Are your sisters caring for you as I commanded?" the king inquired.

Oona was afraid to tell the truth; she thought her sisters would beat her as soon as their father left home again.

Anxious at her silence King Curucha asked Oona what he could do to cheer her spirits.

"I believe I would be happier if my dear Mother Brigid was here," she quietly replied.

"She shall be here within a week," said her father.

He was rewarded with a golden smile that reminded him of his dear wife.

A few days later Oona was called into the courtyard and there she saw her foster mother. As she ran to embrace her, Oona's eyes were so full of happy tears that she did not at first notice the small boy who hid in the folds of Mother Brigid's robes.

"This is Cormac, my only grandson," Mother Brigid told Oona. "His mother died when he was a tiny child, just as yours did. He has no one in the world but me."

"And now you and he are all the world to me," said Oona. "Welcome, little Cormac. Will you be my brother and my friend?"

Oona seemed so kind and gentle, Cormac's loneliness vanished. "I will," he said, and silently he vowed that he would never leave the princess's side.

King Curucha's next journey took him far across the sea. Before he left, he told his elder daughters to take good care of Oona.

"She's frail like her mother," he said, "and I want to see her with roses in her cheeks. Give her a gentle horse and take her riding with you."

Sorcha and Deirdra had other ideas. A cold, cold winter gripped the land. Snow besieged the castle and icicles hung in every window. The sisters made Oona carry frozen branches up the winding stairs, so they would have fires to warm them. But when Oona sighed, a hand was always there to help her. Little Cormac stayed as close as a shadow, playing on a flute to cheer her spirits.

Undaunted by the snow, Sorcha and Deirdra commanded that a path be cleared for their visits to church, where the prince of Ermania awaited them. He had been betrothed to Sorcha, but had never loved her; he had only agreed to the marriage in order to please his ministers and King Curucha.

"If you could go to church with your sisters, what would you choose to wear?" Mother Brigid asked Oona. When the girl just hung her head at the impossibility of such an event, her foster mother declared, "I have a little magic, Oona, and though I cannot give your sisters hearts of gold, with your help I might achieve some small enchantment!"

Oona looked out the window for inspiration. "I would choose a white dress and a white cloak and sky-blue shoes," she said. "And I would ride a snow-white mare with a silver bridle."

Mother Brigid smiled. She went to her old iron chest and brought out a mysteriously glimmering cloak. With a tiny pair of scissors she snipped a corner from Oona's ragged skirt and a thread from her shoes. Then she swung the cloak about her shoulders and slipped away from the castle.

From her window Oona saw something glitter, bright as starlight in the woods, and a bird flew out as though startled by magic.

Before Cormac could finish the merry tune he had begun, there was Mother Brigid in the doorway with a white dress, a white cloak, and a pair of sky-blue shoes.

"Dress yourself quickly, Daughter," she commanded. "Your white mare waits below. Ride to the church, but stop at the gate and do not dismount. When the congregation comes out, you must gallop away as fast as you can!"

Oona did everything her foster mother told her; but when the congregation rose from Mass, she lingered just a little and saw a handsome and somber young man beside her sister. In a flurry of snow she whirled her horse away, wondering at the young man's sadness.

The congregation gasped at the sight of such a beautiful stranger. Some thought the fairies had conjured her out of the weather, but the prince of Ermania found himself smiling.

That evening Deirdra told Oona of the beautiful lady at the church gate. "Sorcha is angry," Deirdra said, "for the prince of Ermania could talk of no one else. She thinks he has been bewitched by the fairy stranger."

"Is that so?" said Oona softly. Her fine clothes were hidden and her snow-white mare had galloped into the hills.

On the following Sunday Oona said, "My dear Mother Brigid, today I must wear the most beautiful dress in the world, yet I cannot think what dress that should be."

Little Cormac, looking through the window, told her, "The snow has all melted and left the grass bright as emeralds. There is a rainbow in the sky, a golden flower beneath our window, and the gray trees are all hung with diamond dew."

"I shall choose a dress of gold," said Oona, "a cloak that holds every color in the rainbow, and shoes as green as emeralds. And, dear Mother Brigid, can you bring me a gray mare with diamond markings and a golden bridle?"

"I know why your eyes are sparkling, Oona," said Mother Brigid. "Everything shall be as perfect as I can make it, yet you must not be hasty. Let the prince see you, but don't let him reach you; true love is not easily won, it must be tested."

Radiant and beautiful Oona rode to church, but now when the congregation gathered on the path, speechless at the sight of her, she could not turn her horse, for the prince of Ermania held her gaze. The young man began to run. Oona jerked the reins and he leapt to reach her, but caught only an emerald-green shoe.

Oona sped away with an ache in her heart.

For nearly a year the prince of Ermania searched Ireland for the owner of the emerald-green shoe. He forgot his duties and he forgot his betrothed. Some said the fairies had stolen his wits. At last he arrived at King Curucha's castle. He was fearful, for he had insulted the king's eldest daughter, yet this was the only place left to seek the girl who filled his dreams.

"How dare you come to me with your ridiculous request!" shouted the king.

"Blame me if you must, Your Majesty," said the prince. "But I did not choose to love. It has caused me weariness and pain. If there is no one here whose foot shall fit the little shoe, then I shall abandon my quest and marry your daughter Sorcha."

The youth's sincerity pacified the king. He allowed all the girls in his castle to enter the great hall for a fitting. Oona slipped in and joined the throng. Even in rags she looked so beautiful, her spiteful sisters could not endure her company. They dragged her to a wooden chest, thrust her inside, and sat on it. Among the hubbub of excitement only one vigilant watcher noticed.

Every girl in the great hall tried to squeeze into the little green shoe, but it soon became obvious that its mysterious owner was not among them.

"Are these all the ladies in your castle?" inquired the despairing prince.

"So I am told," replied the king. "And yet . . . where is your sister Oona?" he asked Sorcha.

"Sick!" she declared. "A dreadful sight!"

"Not true!" cried little Cormac, and he flung himself at the two princesses, pushing them to the floor, where they squealed and kicked like scalded cats.

The lid of the chest was raised from within, and out stepped Oona.

"It is my lady," breathed the prince. He had no need to fit the shoe, for Oona held its partner in her hand.

The king, delighted that the prince had at least chosen one of his daughters, immediately forgave him, and the following week Oona and the prince were married.

The joy of the young couple touched all who saw them, inspiring cooks, musicians, artists, and dressmakers to make this the most glorious wedding ever known in Ireland. Even Deirdra overcame her anger and resentment and appeared in a fine new gown. But Sorcha, speechless with rage, remained in her chamber, dreaming of revenge.

The day after the wedding Oona and the prince set off for Ermania. Little Cormac accompanied them, but Mother Brigid protested that she was too old for such long journeys and would prefer to return to her own fireside.

There was great rejoicing in Ermania, for the people had begun to think their prince would never find the wife he sought. For a year Oona and her husband lived in great happiness. The prince had a little silver flute made for his wife's birthday, and Cormac taught her all the tunes he knew. The long winter evenings were filled with joyful music, but then as spring approached, tidings reached them of another war rumbling across the sea. The young prince knew he must lead his troops into battle, though he could hardly bear to leave his lovely wife. Oona thought her heart would break as she waved farewell to the ship that carried her husband away.

For three long years she had no news of him. Convinced that he had perished, Oona could hardly bring herself to eat. Worn out with grief and nightmares, she wandered the castle in a coarse gray cloak, murmuring at shadows. Even Cormac could not make her smile.

One day a letter arrived. It was from Sorcha. "Dearest Oona," she wrote. "I am truly sorry for the distress I caused you. Prove that you have forgiven me. Let me be with you, for I have heard that loneliness is making you ill and I wish only for your happiness."

"Don't believe her," Cormac cried.

"Little brother, I must," said Oona. "It would be cruel to deny my sister. Why should she write such loving words if she does not mean them?"

Cormac could find no answer to this, but he remained deeply suspicious and resolved never to let Oona out of his sight.

Yet when Sorcha arrived, she seemed changed. She was kind and considerate and especially admired Oona's flute playing. She persuaded Oona to take long walks along the cliff top with her, and begged her sister to entertain her with a tune while they enjoyed the fresh air.

At last word reached Ermania that the prince was alive and on his way home. Almost beside herself with joy, Oona's pale cheeks began to glow and her eyes to shine. On the day before the prince's return Sorcha begged her to take one last walk along the cliff path. As they looked down into the bay, a huge gray whale blew pearly fountains at them.

"Who would have believed such a great creature would swim so close to shore," said Oona. "I'm glad we are safe up here."

"Not so safe," said Sorcha, and she stretched her long fingers toward Oona who was transfixed with fear. "Now, at last I shall have my rightful place," cried Sorcha, and seizing Oona's cloak, she pushed her sister over the cliff. Without a backward glance the wicked girl donned the gray cloak and hastened to the castle.

Hidden in the trees the faithful Cormac had followed his princess, but he was too late to save her. Running to the cliff edge he saw the great sea-creature. "Oh, Whale! Whale! Whale! What has become of my dear sister?" he sobbed.

The whale turned, churning the water to a silvery broth, and from its belly came the sad faint strains of a flute.

"She is alive," Cormac sang, and he ran and ran for a night and a day, until he arrived at his grandmother's house.

"There is only one thing to be done," said Mother Brigid, "but I am old, Cormac, and my strength is fading. You must help me with my starlight cloak, for its magic lies heavily upon me."

Cormac gently wrapped the cloak about his grandmother's shoulders, and when she stepped into the woods, he watched fiery stars glowing in the trees. One burned brighter than all the rest and grew and grew, until from the trees there bounded a great horse blazing like a flame, in its mouth an arrow tipped with silver.

"The prince must pierce the whale's flesh with silver," said Mother Brigid. "Only then will it give up our dear princess. Speed back now, Cormac, on this fiery horse, the last and best of all my enchantments, and give the magic arrow to the prince. There is not a moment to lose, for Oona may not survive the night."

The great flame horse carried Cormac to Ermania within the hour, and there he learned that Sorcha had tricked the prince into accepting that she was his true wife, changed by years of grief. Even his courtiers and servants could not deny it. They had forgotten Oona's features, seeing always a thin girl draped in gray.

Cormac wandered the castle gardens, not knowing what to do, when all at once he came upon a solitary figure, sighing as though he would drown in sorrow. "Oh, where is my true wife? The lady in my chamber is not she. Will no one believe me?"

"I believe you," cried Cormac, running to the prince; and he told his terrible tale.

When the prince heard all that had befallen his princess, he took his bow and the silver-tipped arrow, mounted the flame-bright horse, and then with Cormac behind him, rode to the bay where the great whale basked in moonlight.

Bravely the young man stepped into the water. He lifted his bow, and fitting the magic arrow, cried, "Forgive me, Whale. I mean you no harm, but now you must give up your treasures."

The arrow sped into the air. For a moment it seemed lost in the spangled heavens, and then like a falling star, it dropped onto the whale's back. The sea boiled and glittered as the furious creature hurtled toward the shore. Just when it seemed that he would crush the prince, the whale stopped. He raised his head, opened his jaws, and spewed a shower of jewels upon the beach. Then he swam out to sea where magic arrows couldn't find him.

On the sand, among a hoard of glistening pearls and tiny fish, lay a girl in a white dress. She was holding her silver flute.

The prince drew Oona into his arms. She opened her eyes and smiled. Cormac, overjoyed at their happiness, took up his flute and played such a sparkling air, it roused the birds and set them singing even in the dark.

The joyful clamor woke the castle, and from her window Sorcha saw three people on a horse that burned like the rising sun. Realizing now that her treachery had been discovered, she mounted the fastest horse in the stables and fled back to her father. When King Curucha heard of Sorcha's crime, however, he put his eldest daughter in a tiny boat and sent her far into the ocean. No one ever saw her again.

From that day onward, Oona and her prince were never parted. But Cormac left Ermania on the flame-bright horse and went to care for his grandmother. She gave him her starlight cloak, and sometimes on a summer night you can see him making magic in the sky!